My P.E. Teacher is a NINJA

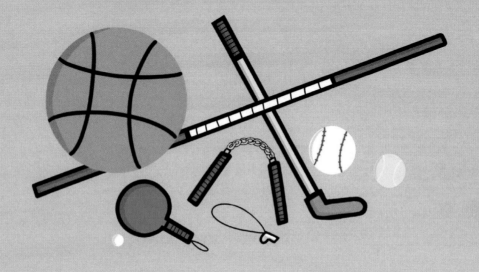

This book is dedicated to my 1,500+
Eagle students over the years.

With love,
Coach Acker

The Wonder Who Crew: Book 1
Copyright © 2018 Joey and Melanie Acker
All rights reserved.
ISBN: 1732745609
ISBN-13: 978-1732745605

My P.E. Teacher is a Ninja

By Joey and Melanie Acker

There's something interesting about my P.E. teacher, Mr. Walker.

We think he might be a ninja.

He can make things disappear.

He teaches us how to roll like a ninja in class.

All of the teachers call for Mr. Walker whenever there is a mouse, snake, or wasp in their room!

We are not sure what happens to them, but we have an idea.

He can tie and untie knots super fast, even double knots!

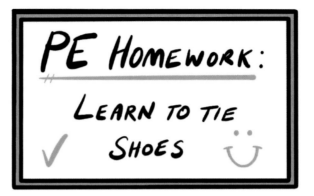

Mr. Walker knows when someone is doing something wrong without looking.

Sometimes we kick our ball over the fence.
He jumps over it to get the ball for us.

He teaches us how to be strong and take care
of our bodies.

Mr. Walker always looks very serious like he is on a secret mission.

But we all know he loves us and wants us to do our best.

OuR GYM PROMISE IS TO ALWAYS

Act SAFELY

Be PREPARED

CooPERATE

Do OuR BEST

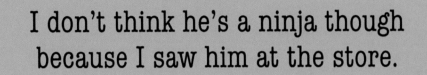

I don't think he's a ninja though because I saw him at the store.

Ninjas don't go to the store.

or do they...